ARSON PLUS

BY

DASHIELL HAMMETT

British Library Cataloguing-in-Publication Data
A catalogue record for this book is available from the
British Library

CONTENTS

DASHIELL HAMMETT

Dashiell Hammett was in Southern Maryland, USA in 1894. He grew up in Philadelphia and Baltimore, before leaving school at thirteen to work with a variety of companies, including the Pinkerton National Detective Agency, with whom he served as an operative between 1915 and 1922. It was the experiences he had while there which provided much of the inspiration for his fiction.

Hammett turned to writing in the twenties – his first published story, 'The Gatewood Caper' (1923), is one of the earliest examples of hardboiled crime fiction – and by the middle of that decade was the pre-eminent writer of detective fiction in America. During the twenties and thirties produced Hammett five novels and a raft of short fiction. Arguably his most successful works – both critically and commercially – are *Red Harvest* (1929), *The Dain Curse* (1929), and *The Glass Key* (1931). *Red Harvest-was* included by *Time* magazine its '100 Best English-language Novels from 1923 to 2005' feature, and Nobel Prize-winning French author André Gide described the novel as "a remarkable achievement, the last word in atrocity, cynicism, and horror."

Hammett's later life was marked in part by ill health, alcoholism, a period of imprisonment related to his alleged

1

membership in the American Communist Party, and by his troubled relationship with his long-time companion, the author Lillian Hellman. He wrote less and less, and by the fifties had become something of a hermit. In 1961, Hammett died in a New York City hospital of lung cancer, diagnosed just two months before. His legacy is formidable: James Ellroy declared that "great crime fiction started with Hammett," and Tony Hillerman called him "the most important American mystery writer of the twentieth century."

ARSON PLUS

Dashiell Hammett

*   *   *

Jim Tarr picked up the cigar I rolled across his desk,
looked at the band, bit off an end, and reached for a match.
'Three for a buck,' he said. 'You must want me to break a
couple of laws for you this time.'
I had been doing business with this fat sheriff of Sacramento County for four or five years—ever since I came
to the Continental Detective Agency's San Francisco
office—and I had never known him to miss an opening for
a sour crack; but it didn't mean anything.
'Wrong both times,' I told him. 'I get them for two bits
each, and I'm here to do you a favour instead of asking for
one. The company that insured Thornburgh's house thinks
somebody touched it off.'
'That's right enough, according to the fire department.
They tell me the lower part of the house was soaked with
gasoline, but the Lord knows how they could tell—there
wasn't a stick left standing. I've got McClump working on
it, but he hasn't found anything to get excited about yet.'
'What's the layout? All I know is that there was a fire.'
Tarr leaned back in his chair, turned his red face to the

ceiling, and bellowed:

'Hey, Mac!'

The pearl push-buttons on his desk are ornaments so far as he is concerned. Deputy sheriffs McHale, McClump and Macklin came to the door together—MacNab apparently wasn't within hearing.

'What's the idea?' the sheriff demanded of McClump.

'Are you carrying a bodyguard around with you?'

The two other deputies, thus informed as to whom 'Mac' referred this time, went back to their cribbage game.

'We got a city slicker here to catch our firebug for us,' Tarr told his deputy. 'But we got to tell him what it's all about first.'

McClump and I had worked together on an express robbery several months before. He's a rangy, tow-headed youngster of twenty-five or six, with all the nerve in the world—and most of the laziness.

'Ain't the Lord good to us?'

He had himself draped across a chair by now—always his first objective when he comes into a room.

'Well, here's how she stands: this fellow Thornburgh's house was a couple miles out of town, on the old county road—and old frame house. About midnight, night before last, Jeff Pringle—the nearest neighbour, a half-mile or so to the east—saw a glare in the sky from over that way, and phoned in the alarm; but by the time the fire wagons got there, there wasn't enough of the house left to bother about. Pringle was the first of the neighbours to get to the house, and the roof had already fallen in then.

'Nobody saw anything suspicious—no strangers hanging around or nothing. Thornburgh's help just managed to save themselves, and that was all. They don't know much about what happened—too scared, I reckon. But they did see Thornburgh at his window just before the fire got him. A fellow here in town—name of Henderson—saw that part of it too. He was driving home from Wayton, and got to the house just before the roof caved in.

'The fire department people say they found signs of gasoline. The Coonses, Thornburgh's help, say they didn't have no gas on the place. So there you are.'

'Thornburgh have any relatives?'

'Yeah. A niece in San Francisco—a Mrs Evelyn Trowbridge. She was up yesterday, but there wasn't nothing she could do, and she couldn't tell us nothing much, so she went home.'

'Where are the servants now?'

'Here in town. Staying at a hotel on I Street. I told 'em to stick around for a few days.'

'Thornburgh own the house?'

'Uh-huh. Bought it from Newning & Weed a couple months ago.'

'You got anything to do this morning?'

'Nothing but this.'

'Good. Let's get out and dig around.'

We found the Coonses in their room at the hotel on I Street. Mr Coons was a small-boned, plump man with the smooth, meaningless face, and the suavity of the typical male house-servant.

His wife was a tall, stringy woman, perhaps five years older than her husband—say, forty—with a mouth and chin that seemed shaped for gossiping. But he did all the talking, while she nodded her agreement to every second or third word.

'We went to work for Mr Thornburgh on the fifteenth of

June, I think,' he said, in reply to my first question. 'We
came to Sacramento around the first of the month, and put
in applications at the Allis Employment Bureau. A couple
of weeks later they sent us out to see Mr Thornburgh, and
he took us on.'

'Where were you before you came here?'

'In Seattle, sir, with a Mrs Comerford; but the climate
there didn't agree with my wife—she has bronchial trouble—so we decided to come to California. We most likely
would have stayed in Seattle, though, if Mrs Comerford
hadn't given up her house.'

'What do you know about Thornburgh?'

'Very little, sir. He wasn't a talkative gentleman. He
hadn't any business that I know of. I think he was a retired
seafaring man. He never said he was, but he had that manner and look. He never went out or had anybody in to see
him, except his niece once, and he didn't write or get any
mail. He had a room next to his bedroom fixed up as a sort
of workshop. He spent most of his time in there. I always
thought he was working on some kind of invention, but he
kept the door locked, and wouldn't let us go near it.'

'Haven't you any idea at all what it was?'

'No, sir. We never heard any hammering or noises from it,
and never smelled anything either. And none of his clothes
were ever the least bit soiled, even when they were ready
to go out to the laundry. They would have been if he had
been working on anything like machinery.'

'Was he an old man?'

'He couldn't have been over fifty, sir. He was very erect,
and his hair and beard were thick, with no grey hairs.'

'Ever have any trouble with him?'

'Oh, no, sir! He was, if I may say it, a very peculiar gentleman in a way; and he didn't care about anything except having his meals fixed right, having his clothes taken care of—he was very particular about them—and not being disturbed. Except early in the morning and at night, we'd hardly see him all day.'

'Now about the fire. Tell us the whole thing—everything you remember.'

'Well, sir, my wife and I had gone to bed about ten o'clock, our regular time, and had gone to sleep. Our room was on the second floor, in the rear. Some time later—I never did exactly know what time it was—I woke up, coughing. The room was all full of smoke, and my wife was sort of strangling. I jumped up, and dragged her down the back stairs and out the back door, not thinking of anything but getting her out of there.

'When I had her safe in the yard, I thought of Mr Thornburgh, and tried to get back in the house; but the whole first floor was just flames. I ran around front then, to see if he had got out, but didn't see anything of him. The whole yard was as light as day by then. Then I heard him scream—a horrible scream, sir—I can hear it yet! And I looked up at his window—that was the front second-storey room—and saw him there, trying to get out the window. But all the woodwork was burning, and he screamed again and fell back, and right after that the roof over his room fell in.

'There wasn't a ladder or anything that I could have put up to the window for him—there wasn't anything I could have done.

'In the meantime, a gentleman had left his automobile in the road, and come up to where I was standing; but there wasn't anything we could do—the house was burning everywhere and falling in here and there. So we went back to where I had left my wife, and carried her farther away from the fire, and brought her to—she had fainted. And that's all I know about it, sir.'

'Hear any noises earlier that night? Or see anybody hanging around?'

'No, sir.'

'Have any gasoline around the place?'

'No, sir. Mr Thornburgh didn't have a car.'

'No gasoline for cleaning?'

'No, sir, none at all, unless Mr Thornburgh had it in his workshop. When his clothes needed cleaning, I took them to town, and all his laundry was taken by the grocer's man, when he brought our provisions.'

'Don't know anything that might have some bearing on the fire?'

'No, sir. I was surprised when I heard that somebody had set the house afire. I could hardly believe it. I don't know why anybody should want to do that . . .'

'What do you think of them?' I asked McClump, as we left the hotel.

'They might pad the bills, or even go South with some of the silver, but they don't figure as killers in my mind.'

That was my opinion, too; but they were the only persons known to have been there when the fire started except the man who had died. We went around to the Allis Employment Bureau and talked to the manager.

He told us that the Coonses had come into his office on June second, looking for work; and had given Mrs Edward Comerford, 45 Wood-mansee Terrace, Seattle, Washington, as reference. In reply to a letter—he always checked up the references of servants—Mrs Comerford had writ-

ten that the Coonses had been in her employ for a number
of years, and had been 'extremely satisfactory in every
respect.' On June thirteenth, Thornburgh had telephoned
the bureau, asking that a man and his wife be sent out to
keep house for him, and Allis sent out two couples he had
listed. Neither couple had been employed by Thornburgh,
though Allis considered them more desirable than the
Coonses, who were finally hired by Thornburgh.

All that would certainly seem to indicate that the Coonses
hadn't deliberately manoeuvred themselves into the place,
unless they were the luckiest people in the world—and a
detective can't afford to believe in luck or coincidence,
unless he has unquestionable proof of it.

At the office of the real-estate agents, through whom
Thornburgh had bought the house—Newning & Weed—
we were told that Thornburgh had come in on the eleventh
of June, and had said that he had been told that the house
was for sale, had looked it over, and wanted to know the
price. The deal had been closed the next morning, and he
had paid for the house with a cheque for $14,500 on the
Seamen's Bank of San Francisco. The house was already
furnished.

After luncheon, McClump and I called on Howard Henderson—the man who had seen the fire while driving home
from Wayton. He had an office in the Empire Building,
with his name and the title *Northern California Agent for
Krispy Korn Krumbs* on the door. He was a big, careless-
looking man of forty-five or so, with the professionally
jovial smile that belongs to the travelling salesman.

He had been in Wayton on business the day of the fire,
he said, and had stayed there until rather late, going to
dinner and afterwards playing pool with a grocer named

Hammersmith—one of his customers. He had left Wayton in his machine, at about ten-thirty, and set out for Sacramento. At Tavender he had stopped at the garage for oil and gas, and to have one of his tyres blown up.

Just as he was about to leave the garage, the garage man had called his attention to a red glare in the sky, and had told him that it was probably from a fire somewhere along the old county road that paralleled the State Road into Sacramento; so Henderson had taken the county road, and had arrived at the burning house just in time to see Thornburgh try to fight his way through the flames.

It was too late to make any attempt to put out the fire, and the man upstairs was beyond saving by then—undoubtedly dead even before the roof collapsed; so Henderson had helped Coons revive his wife, and stayed there watching the fire until it had burned itself out. He had seen no one on that county road while driving to the fire . . .

'What do you know about Henderson?' I asked McClump, when we were on the street.

'Came here, from somewhere in the East, I think, early in the summer to open that breakfast cereal agency. Lives at the Garden Hotel. Where do we go next?'

'We get a car, and take a look at what's left of the Thornburgh house.'

An enterprising incendiary couldn't have found a lovelier spot in which to turn himself loose, if he looked the whole county over. Tree-topped hills hid it from the rest of the world, on three sides; while away from the fourth, an uninhabited plain rolled down to the river. The county road that passed the front gate was shunned by automobiles, so McClump said, in favour of the State Highway to the north.

Where the house had been was now a mound of blackened ruins. We poked around in the ashes for a few minutes— not that we expected to find anything, but because it's the nature of man to poke around in ruins.

A garage in the rear, whose interior gave no evidence of recent occupation, had a badly scorched roof and front, but was otherwise undamaged. A shed behind it, sheltering an axe, a shovel, and various odds and ends of gardening tools, had escaped the fire altogether. The lawn in front of the house, and the garden behind the shed—about an acre in all—had been pretty thoroughly cut and trampled by wagon wheels, and the feet of the firemen and the spectators.

Having ruined our shoe-shines, McClump and I got back in our car and swung off in a circle around the place, calling at all the houses within a mile radius, and getting little besides jolts for our trouble.

The nearest house was that of Pringle, the man who had turned in the alarm; but he not only knew nothing about the dead man, he said he had never even seen him. In fact, only one of the neighbours had ever seen him: a Mrs Jabine, who lived about a mile to the south.

She had taken care of the key to the house while it was vacant; and a day or two before he bought it, Thornburgh had come to her house, enquiring about the vacant one. She had gone over there with him and shown him through it, and he had told her that he intended buying it, if the price, of which neither of them knew anything, wasn't too high.

He had been alone, except for the chauffeur of the hired car in which he had come from Sacramento, and, save that he had no family, he had told her nothing about himself.

11

Hearing that he had moved in, she went over to call on
him several days later—'just a neighbourly visit'—but had
been told by Mrs Coons that he was not at home. Most
of the neighbours had talked to the Coonses, and had got
the impression that Thornburgh did not care for visitors,
so they had let him alone. The Coonses were described as
'pleasant enough to talk to when you meet them', but re-
flecting their employer's desire not to make friends.
McClump summarised what the afternoon had taught us
as we pointed our car towards Tavender: 'Any of these
folks could have touched off the place, but we got nothing
to show that any of 'em even knew Thornburgh, let alone
had a bone to pick with him.'
Tavender turned out to be a crossroads settlement of a
general store and post office, a garage, a church, and six
dwellings, about two miles from Thornburgh's place. Mc-
Clump knew the storekeeper and postmaster, a scrawny
little man named Philo, who stuttered moistly.
'I n-n-never s-saw Th-thornburgh,' he said, 'and I n-n-never had any m-mail for him. C-coons'—it sounded like one
of these things butterflies come out of—'used to c-come
in once a week t-to order groceries—they d-didn't have a
phone. He used to walk in, and I'd s-send the stuff over in
my c-c-car. Th-then I'd s-see him once in a while, waiting
f-for the stage to S-s-sacramento.'
'Who drove the stuff out to Thornburgh's?'
'M-m-my b-boy. Want to t-talk to him?'
The boy was a juvenile edition of the old man, but without
the stutter. He had never seen Thornburgh on any of his
visits, but his business had taken him only as far as the
kitchen. He hadn't noticed anything peculiar about the
place.

12

'Who's the night man at the garage?' I asked him.
'Billy Luce. I think you can catch him there now. I saw
him go in a few minutes ago.'
We crossed the road and found Luce.
'Night before last—the night of the fire down the road—
was there a man here talking to you when you first saw it?'
He turned his eyes upward in that vacant stare which peo-
ple use to aid their memory.
'Yes, I remember now! He was going to town, and I told
him that if he took the county road instead of the State
Road he'd see the fire on his way in.'
'What kind of looking man was he?'
'Middle-aged—a big man, but sort of slouchy. I think he
had on a brown suit, baggy and wrinkled.'
'Medium complexion?'
'Yes.'
'Smile when he talked?'
'Yes, a pleasant sort of fellow.'
'Brown hair?'
'Yeah, but have a heart!' Luce laughed. 'I didn't put him
under a magnifying glass.'
From Tavender we drove over to Wayton. Luce's descrip-
tion had fit Henderson all right, but while we were at it,
we thought we might as well check up to make sure that
he had been coming from Wayton.
We spent exactly twenty-five minutes in Wayton; ten of
them finding Hammersmith, the grocer with whom Hend-
erson had said he dined and played pool; five minutes
finding the proprietor of the pool room; and ten verifying
Henderson's story . . .
'What do you think of it now, Mac?' I asked, as we rolled
back towards Sacramento.

Mac's too lazy to express an opinion, or even form one, unless he's driven to it; but that doesn't mean they aren't worth listening to.

'There ain't a hell of a lot to think,' he said cheerfully. 'Henderson is out of it, if he ever was in it. There's nothing to show that anybody but the Coonses and Thornburgh were there when the fire started—but there may have been a regiment there. Them Coonses ain't too honest-looking, maybe, but they ain't killers, or I miss my guess. But the fact remains that they're the only bet we got so far. Maybe we ought to try to get a line on them.'

'All right,' I agreed. 'Soon as we get back to town, I'll get a wire off to our Seattle office asking them to interview Mrs Comerford, and see what she can tell about them. Then I'm going to catch a train for San Francisco and see Thornburgh's niece in the morning.'

Next morning, at the address McClump had given me—a rather elaborate apartment building on California Street—I had to wait three-quarters of an hour for Mrs Evelyn Trowbridge to dress. If I had been younger, or a social caller, I suppose I'd have felt amply rewarded when she finally came in—a tall, slender woman of less than thirty; in some sort of clinging black affair; with a lot of black hair over a very white face, strikingly set off by a small red mouth and big hazel eyes that looked black until you got close to them.

But I was a busy, middle-aged detective, who was fuming over having his time wasted; and I was a lot more interested in finding the bird who struck the match than I was in feminine beauty. However, I smothered my grouch, apologised for disturbing her at such an early hour, and got down to business.

'I want you to tell me all you know about your uncle—his family, friends, enemies, business connections—everything.'

I had scribbled on the back of the card I had sent in to her what my business was.

'He hadn't any family,' she said; 'unless I might be it. He was my mother's brother, and I am the only one of that family now living.'

'Where was he born?'

'Here in San Francisco. I don't know the date, but he was about fifty years old, I think—three years older than my mother.'

'What was his business?'

'He went to sea when he was a boy, and, so far as I know, always followed it until a few months ago.'

'Captain?'

'I don't know. Sometimes I wouldn't see or hear from him for several years, and he never talked about what he was doing; though he would mention some of the places he had visited—Rio de Janeiro, Madagascar, Tobago, Christiania. Then, about three months ago—some time in May—he came here and told me that he was through with wandering; that he was going to take a house in some quiet place where he could work undisturbed on an invention in which he was interested.

'He lived at the Francisco Hotel while he was in San Francisco. After a couple of weeks he suddenly disappeared. And then, about a month ago, I received a telegram from him, asking me to come to see him at his house near Sacramento. I went up the very next day, and I thought that he was acting queerly—he seemed very excited over something. He gave me a will that he had just drawn up and

some life insurance policies in which I was beneficiary.
'Immediately after that he insisted that I return home, and
hinted rather plainly that he did not wish me to either visit
him again or write until I heard from him. I thought all
that rather peculiar, as he had always seemed fond of me. I
never saw him again.'

'What was this invention he was working on?'

'I really don't know. I asked him once, but he became so
excited—even suspicious—that I changed the subject, and
never mentioned it again.'

'Are you sure that he really did follow the sea all those
years?'

'No, I am not. I just took it for granted; but he may have
been doing something altogether different.'

'Was he ever married?'

'Not that I know of.'

'Know any of his friends or enemies?'

'No, none.'

'Remember anybody's name that he ever mentioned?'

'No.'

'I don't want you to think this next question insulting,
though I admit it is. But it has to be asked. Where were
you on the night of the fire?'

'At home; I had some friends here to dinner, and they
stayed until about midnight. Mr and Mrs Walker Kellogg,
Mrs John Dupree, and a Mr Killmer, who is a lawyer. I
can give you their addresses, or you can get them from the
phone book, if you want to question them.'

From Mrs Trowbridge's apartment I went to the Francisco
Hotel. Thornburgh had been registered there from May
tenth to June thirteenth, and hadn't attracted much attention. He had been a tall, broad-shouldered, erect man of

about fifty, with rather long brown hair brushed straight
back; a short, pointed, brown beard, and healthy, ruddy
complexion—grave, quiet, punctilious in dress and manner; his hours had been regular and he had had no visitors
that any of the hotel employees remembered.

At the Seamen's Bank—upon which Thornburgh's
cheque, in payment of the house, had been drawn—I was
told that he had opened an account there on May fifteenth,
having been introduced by W. W. Jeffers & Sons, local
stock brokers. A balance of a little more than four hundred
dollars remained to his credit. The cancelled cheques on
hand were all to the order of various life insurance companies; and for amounts that, if they represented premiums,
testified to rather large policies. I jotted down the names of
the life insurance companies, and then went to the office
of W. W. Jeffers & Sons.

Thornburgh had come in, I was told, on the tenth of May
with $ 15,000 worth of bonds that he wanted sold. Dur-
ing one of his conversations with Jeffers he had asked the
broker to recommend a bank, and Jeffers had given him a
letter to the Seamen's Bank.

That was all Jeffers knew about him. He gave me the
numbers of the bonds, but tracing bonds isn't always the
easiest thing in the world.

The reply to my Seattle telegram was waiting for me at the
Continental Detective Agency when I arrived.

MRS EDWARD COMERFORD RENTED APARTMENT
AT ADDRESS YOU GIVE ON MAY TWENTY-FIVE.
GAVE IT UP JUNE SIX. TRUNKS TO SAN FRANCIS-
CO SAME DAY. CHECK NUMBERS GN FOUR FIVE
TWO FIVE EIGHT SEVEN AND EIGHT AND NINE

Tracing baggage is no trick at all, if you have the dates
and check numbers to start with—as many a bird who is
wearing somewhat similar numbers on his chest and back,
because he overlooked that detail when making his geta-
way, can tell you—and twenty-five minutes in a baggage-
room at the ferry and half an hour in the office of a trans-
fer company gave me my answer.
The trunks had been delivered to Mrs Evelyn Trowbridge's
apartment!
I got Jim Tarr on the phone.
'Good shooting!' he said, forgetting for once to indulge
his wit. 'We'll grab the Coonses here and Mrs Trowbridge
there, and that's the end of another mystery.'
'Wait a minute!' I cautioned him. 'It's not all straightened
out yet—there's still a few kinks in the plot.'
'It's straight enough for me. I'm satisfied.'
'You're the boss, but I think you're being a little hasty.
I'm going up to talk with the niece again. Give me a little
time before you phone the police here to make the pinch.
I'll hold her until they get there.'

*

Evelyn Trowbridge let me in this time, instead of the maid
who had opened the door for me in the morning, and she
led me to the same room in which we had had our first
talk. I let her pick out a seat, and then I selected one that
was closer to either door than hers was.

18

On the way up I had planned a lot of innocent-sounding questions that would get her all snarled up; but after taking a good look at this woman sitting in front of me, leaning comfortably back in her chair, coolly waiting for me to speak my piece, I discarded the trick stuff and came out cold-turkey.

'Ever use the name Mrs Edward Comerford?'

'Oh, yes.' As casual as a nod on the street.

'When?'

'Often. You see, I happen to have been married not so long ago to Mr Edward Comerford. So it's not really strange that I should have used the name.'

'Use it in Seattle recently?'

'I would suggest,' she said sweetly, 'that if you are leading up to the references I gave Coons and his wife, you might save time by coming right to it?'

'That's fair enough,' I said. 'Let's do that.'

There wasn't a tone or shading, in voice, manner, or expression, to indicate that she was talking about anything half so serious or important to her as a possibility of being charged with murder. She might have been talking about the weather, or a book that hadn't interested her particularly.

'During the time that Mr Comerford and I were married, we lived in Seattle, where he still lives. After the divorce, I left Seattle and resumed my maiden name. And the Coonses *were* in our employ, as you might learn if you care to look it up. You'll find my husband—or former husband—at the Chelsea apartments.

'Last summer, or late spring, I decided to return to Seattle. The truth of it is—I suppose all my personal affairs will be aired anyhow—that I thought perhaps Edward and I might patch up our differences; so I went back and took an apartment on Woodmansee Terrace. As I was known in Seattle as Mrs Edward Comerford, and as I thought my using his name might influence him a little, I used it while I was there.

'Also I telephoned the Coonses to make tentative arrangements in case Edward and I should open our house again; but Coons told me that they were going to California, and so I gladly gave them an excellent recommendation when, some days later, I received a letter of enquiry from an employment bureau in Sacramento. After I had been in Seattle for about two weeks, I changed my mind about the reconciliation—Edward's interest, I learned, was all centred elsewhere; so I returned to San Francisco—'

'Very nice! But—'

'If you will permit me to finish,' she interrupted. 'When I went to see my uncle in response to his telegram, I was surprised to find the Coonses in his house. Knowing my uncle's peculiarities, and finding them now increased, and remembering his extreme secretiveness about his mysterious invention, I cautioned the Coonses not to tell him that they had been in my employ.

'He certainly would have discharged them, and just as certainly would have quarrelled with me—he would have thought that I was having him spied on. Then, when Coons telephoned me after the fire, I knew that to admit that the Coonses had been formerly in my employ would, in view of the fact that I was my uncle's only heir, cast suspicion on all three of us. So we foolishly agreed to say nothing about it and carry on the deception.'

That didn't sound all wrong—but it didn't sound all right. I wished Tarr had taken it easier and let us get a better line

on these people, before having them thrown in the coop.
'The coincidence of the Coonses stumbling into my uncle's house is, I fancy, too much for your detecting in-
stincts,' she went on, as I didn't say anything. 'Am I to
consider myself under arrest?'

I'm beginning to like this girl; she's a nice, cool piece of
work.

'Not yet,' I told her. 'But I'm afraid it's going to happen
pretty soon.'

She smiled a little mocking smile at that, and another
when the doorbell rang.

It was O'Hara from police headquarters. We turned the
apartment upside down and inside out, but didn't find anything of importance except the will she had told me about,
dated July eighth, and her uncle's life insurance policies.
They were all dated between May fifteenth and June tenth,
and added up to a little more than $200,000.

I spent an hour grilling the maid after O'Hara had taken
Evelyn Trowbridge away, but she didn't know any more
than I did. However, between her, the janitor, the manager
of the apartments, and the names Mrs Trowbridge had
given me, I learned that she had really been entertaining
friends on the night of the fire—until after eleven o'clock,
anyway—and that was late enough.

Half an hour later I was riding the Short Line back to Sacramento. I was getting to be one of the line's best customers, and my anatomy was on bouncing terms with every
bump in the road!

Between bumps I tried to fit the pieces of this Thornburgh puzzle together. The niece and the Coonses fitted
in somewhere, but not just where we had them. We had
been working on the job sort of lopsided, but it was the

best we could do with it. In the beginning we had turned to the Coonses and Evelyn Trowbridge because there was no other direction to go; and now we had something on them—but a good lawyer could make hash out of it.

The Coonses were in the county jail when I got to Sacramento. After some questioning they had admitted their connection with the niece, and had come through with stories that matched hers in every detail.

Tarr, McClump and I sat around the sheriff's desk and argued.

'Those yarns are pipe dreams,' the sheriff said. 'We got all three of 'em cold, and there's nothing else to it. They're as good as convicted.'

McClump grinned derisively at his superior, and then turned to me.

'Go on, you tell him about the holes in his little case. He ain't your boss, and can't take it out on you later for being smarter than he is!'

Tarr glared from one of us to the other.

'Spill it, you wise guys!' he ordered.

'Our dope is,' I told him, figuring that McClump's view of it was the same as mine, 'that there's nothing to show that even Thornburgh knew he was going to buy that house before the tenth of June, and that the Coonses were in town looking for work on the second. And besides, it was only by luck that they got the jobs. The employment office sent two couples out there ahead of them.'

'We'll take a chance on letting the jury figure that out.'

'Yes? You'll also take a chance on them figuring out that Thornburgh, who seems to have been a nut, might have touched off the place himself! We've got something on these people, Jim, but not enough to go into court with them. How are you going to prove that when the Coonses were planted in Thornburgh's house—if you can even prove that they and the Trowbridge woman knew he was going to load up with insurance policies?'

The sheriff spat disgustedly.

'You guys are the limit! You run around in circles, digging up the dope on these people until you get enough to hang 'em, and then you run around hunting for outs! What's the matter with you now?'

I answered him from halfway to the door—the pieces were beginning to fit together under my skull.

'Going to run some more circles—come on, Mac!'

McClump and I held a conference on the fly, and then I got a car from the nearest garage and headed for Tavender. We made time going out, and got there before the general store had closed for the night. The stuttering Philo separated himself from the two men with whom he had been talking, and followed me to the rear of the store.

'Do you keep an itemised list of the laundry you handle?'

'N-n-no; just the amounts.'

'Let's look at Thornburgh's.'

He produced a begrimed and rumpled account book, and we picked out the weekly items I wanted: $2.60, $3.10, $2.25, and so on.

'Got the last batch of laundry here?'

'Y-yes,' he said. 'It j-just c-c-came out from the city t-today.'

I tore open the bundle—some sheets, pillowcases, table-cloths, towels, napkins; some feminine clothing; some shirts, collars, underwear, and socks that were unmistakably Coons's. I thanked Philo while running back to the car. Back in Sacramento again, McClump was waiting for me

23

at the garage where I had hired the car.

'Registered at the hotel on June fifteenth, rented the office on the sixteenth. I think he's in the hotel now,' he greeted me.

We hurried around the block to the Garden Hotel.

'Mr Henderson went out a minute or two ago,' the night clerk told us. 'He seemed to be in a hurry.'

'Know where he keeps his car?'

'In the hotel garage around the corner.'

We were within ten feet of the garage, when Henderson's automobile shot out and turned up the street.

'Oh, Mr Henderson!' I cried, trying to keep my voice level.

He stepped on the gas and streaked away from us.

'Want him?' McClump asked; and at my nod he stopped a passing roadster by the simple expedient of stepping in front of it.

We climbed in, McClump flashed his star at the bewildered driver, and pointed out Henderson's dwindling tail-light. After he had persuaded himself that he wasn't being boarded by a couple of bandits, the commandeered driver did his best, and we picked up Henderson's tail-light after two or three turnings, and closed in on him—though his car was going at a good clip.

By the time we reached the outskirts of the city, we had crawled up to within safe shooting distance, and I sent a bullet over the fleeing man's head. Thus encouraged, he managed to get a little more speed out of his car; but we were definitely overhauling him now.

Just at the wrong minute Henderson decided to look over his shoulder at us—an unevenness in the road twisted his wheels—his machine swayed—skidded—went over on its side. Almost immediately, from the heart of the tangle, came a flash and a bullet moaned past my ear. Another. And then, while I was still hunting for something to shoot at in the pile of junk we were drawing down upon, Mc-Clump's ancient and battered revolver roared in my other ear.

Henderson was dead when we got to him—McClump's bullet had taken him over one eye.

McClump said over the body:

'I ain't an inquisitive sort of fellow, but I hope you don't mind telling me why I shot this lad.'

'Because he was—*Thornburgh.*'

He didn't say anything for about five minutes. Then: 'I reckon that's right. How'd you know it?'

We were sitting beside the wreckage now, waiting for the police that we had sent our commandeered chauffeur to phone for.

'He had to be,' I said, 'when you think it all over. Funny we didn't hit on it before! All that stuff we were told about Thornburgh had a fishy sound. Whiskers and an unknown profession, immaculate and working on a mysterious invention, very secretive and born in San Francisco—where the fire wiped out all the old records—just the sort of fake that could be cooked up easily.

'Now, consider Henderson. You had told me he came to Sacramento sometime early this summer—and the dates you got tonight show that he didn't come until *after* Thornburgh had bought his house. All right! Now compare Henderson with the descriptions we got of Thornburgh.

'Both are about the same size and age, and with the same colour hair. The differences are all things that can be manufactured—clothes, a little sunburn, and a month's growth of beard, along with a little acting, would do the trick. Tonight I went out to Tavender and took a look at the last batch of laundry—*and there wasn't any that didn't fit the Coonses!* And none of the bills all the way back were large enough for Thornburgh to have been as careful about his clothes as we were told he was.'

'It must be great to be a detective!' McClump grinned as the police ambulance came up and began disgorging policemen. 'I reckon somebody must have tipped Henderson off that I was asking about him this evening.' And then, regretfully: 'So we ain't going to hang them folks for murder after all.'

'No, but we oughtn't have any trouble convicting them of arson plus conspiracy to defraud, and anything else that the Prosecuting Attorney can think up.'